VILLA PARK PUBLIC LIBRARY

3 27 2 00118 6574

P9-AOZ-581

WID
3509

Villa Park Public Library
Villa Park, Illinois
Phone No. 834-1164

FLY AWAY!

BY HELEN and KELLY OECHSLI

Macmillan Publishing Company   New York
Collier Macmillan Publishers   London

VILLA PARK PUBLIC LIBRARY

E (PIC)
Oec

Copyright © 1988 by Helen Oechsli and Kelly Oechsli. All rights reserved. No part of this book
may be reproduced or transmitted in any form or by any means, electronic or mechanical,
including photocopying, recording, or by any information storage and retrieval system, without
permission in writing from the Publisher. Macmillan Publishing Company, 866 Third Avenue,
New York, NY 10022. Collier Macmillan Canada, Inc.

Printed and bound in Japan. First American Edition.

10 9 8 7 6 5 4 3 2 1

The text of this book is set in 13 point Auriga.
The illustrations are rendered in pen-and-ink and watercolor.

Library of Congress Cataloging-in-Publication Data. Oechsli, Helen. Fly away! Summary:
A little girl takes her first airplane ride with her parents to visit her grandparents. [1. Airplanes –
Fiction] I. Oechsli, Kelly. II. Title. PZ7.O26Fl 1988 [E] 88-4295
ISBN 0-02-768520-9

*M*ommy just said we're flying to visit Gram and Grampa! I know I'll like flying … flying….

Oh, Gypsy, I wish you could come. But Uncle Paul
will take good care of you.

Only one suitcase for me. What
shall I take? There's not much
room on a plane.

This dress, that doll.
Oh, it's hard to choose.

Don't be sad, Gypsy. We'll be
back.

What a funny car. Or is it a bus?
Are those people going to the
airport too?

Mommy says this line is going to
Gram and Grampa's, Bear. Don't
worry!

Our suitcases are riding off on a moving belt.
Daddy says the belt takes them to "the belly of the
plane."

How do we get them back after the plane swallows
them? Our names are on them, but I'm keeping you
with me, Bear.

That's silly! A doorway to walk through, standing
all by itself, and a tunnel for bags and you too, Bear,
to ride through.

Here you come, out again.
Daddy says with the door and the
tunnel they can see inside
everything to make sure we're safe.
They must be taking good care of
us. Did you like the ride, Bear?

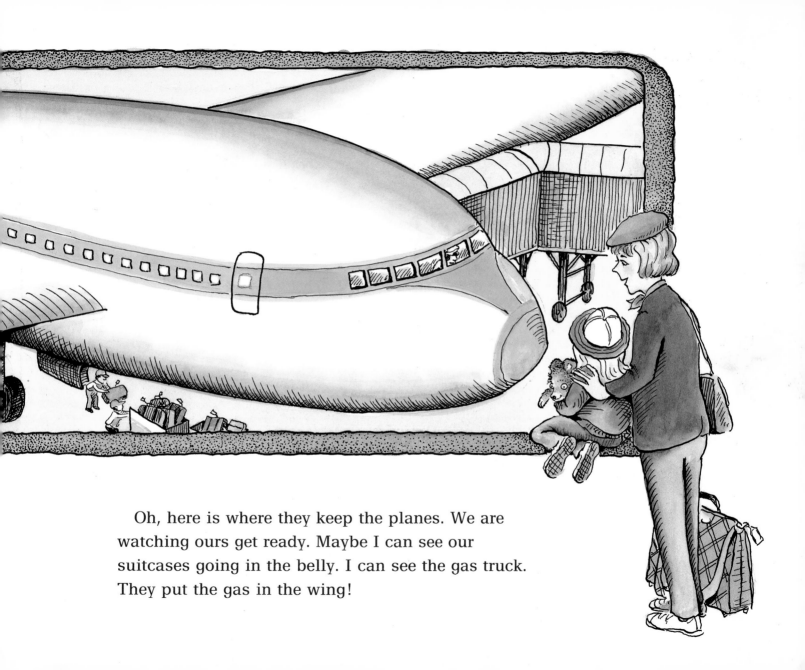

Oh, here is where they keep the planes. We are
watching ours get ready. Maybe I can see our
suitcases going in the belly. I can see the gas truck.
They put the gas in the wing!

Now our plane is ready for us.
It doesn't look like a plane from
here. Are you sure this is it,
Daddy?

Here we are inside! It looks something like a big
bus. The driver sits up there in front. They call him
the pilot. Oh, I hope I can sit near a window. There's
so much to look at.

We're all ready. We have our seat belts on. I'll hold you, Bear. That lady walking up and down is a flight attendant. Mommy says that she will take good care of us on the plane. Listen! They're telling us everything to do. It sounds like a radio, but it's a loudspeaker.

Hold on tight. Here we go! Faster, faster, and what
a loud motor. Oh—we are going up. Bear, we're really
flying! Aren't you excited, Bear?

VILLA PARK PUBLIC LIBRARY

Just look! Tiny cars, like toys. I can't see people anymore. There's our big river. See the bridge? My ears feel funny.

It's a long way to Gram and Grampa's, so they're giving us dinner. We all have our own little tables! Are you hungry, Bear?

Look at those trays she is handing us. I see
potatoes and meat. Why, it's a regular meal.
Don't worry, Bear. I'll give you some of mine.

It's all right for us to walk in the aisle to the bathroom. Look how tiny it is, and everything works! Can you believe it?

Daddy is getting earphones. They plug into the arm of his seat, and he can listen to music. Not me. There's too much to see.

We can make our seats go back. Mommy says, Take a nap. I don't feel sleepy. Do you, Bear?

Bear, I hear the pilot on the loudspeaker. He says
we're getting ready to land. We're almost there.
Those are real mountains. No more white clouds.

Fasten our seat belts! Now we're going down.
My ears are popping again. Hold tight!

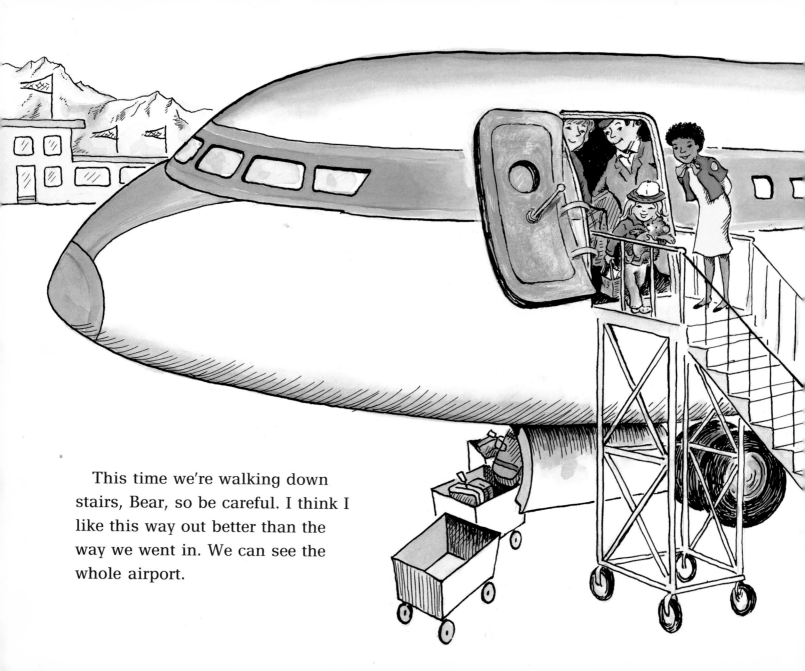

This time we're walking down stairs, Bear, so be careful. I think I like this way out better than the way we went in. We can see the whole airport.

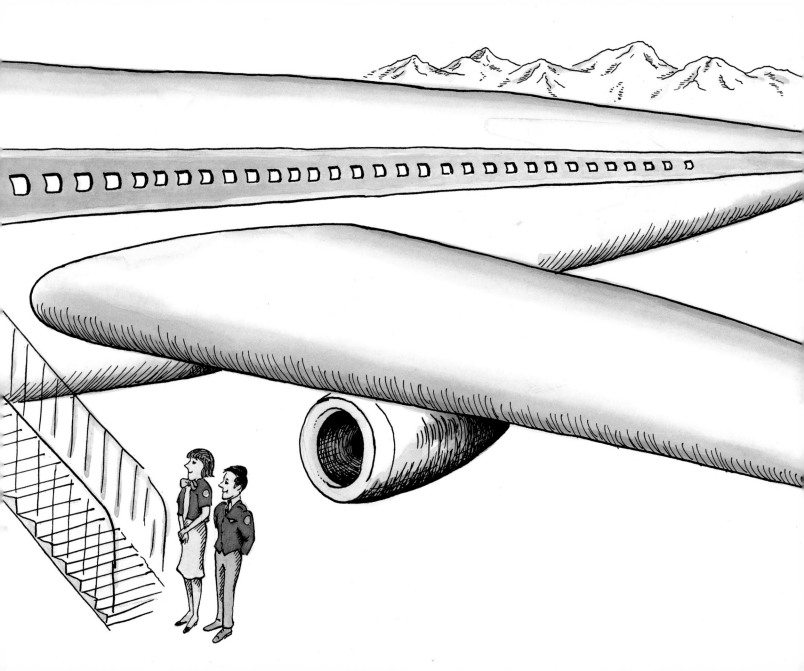

I see Gram and Grampa! I see
them! Over there, Bear. Hello!
Hello!

Will we find our suitcases? Grampa says they'll
come by. All we have to do is wait.

Do we look any different, Gram? We've been flying,
you know.